Also by Rachael Reed

Codefendant
Codefendant
Once a Cheater
Once a Cheater
Passport Bro
What Happens in Prison
Preference
Sprinkle Sprinkle
Championship Bad
Street Exodus
Street Exodus
Street Royalty
Pawns of Power
SIS
Cartel Bloodline
Get Money Girls
Skip the Games
Til Death Do Us Part
Backpage Hustle
Link in Bio
The Virgin and The Kingpin
A Gangsta's Heart

A Gangta's Heart

Rachael Reed
©2024

A Gangsta's Heart

By Rachael Reed

Copyright © 2024 by Rachael Reed

Check Out More Great Products and Free Giveaways

https://tbdbpublishing.com/

All rights reserved. No part of this publication may be reproduced, Resold, distributed, or transmitted in any form or by any means, including photocopying, recording, or other electronic or otherwise

Chapter 1: The Return

Ranisha Barlow stepped off the bus, the familiar sights and sounds of her old neighborhood assaulting her senses. The worn streets, the sagging power lines, the graffiti-tagged walls—it was all just as she remembered, yet it felt like a lifetime had passed since she last walked these streets. With a duffel bag slung over her shoulder, she took a deep breath, steeling herself for what was to come.

Ranisha had always been different. From a young age, she knew she was destined for more than what the hood had to offer. Her mother had worked tirelessly to put food on the table, often holding down two jobs, while her father was in and out of prison. Despite the chaos around her, Ranisha found solace in her books. She excelled in school, her academic achievements providing a glimmer of hope in an otherwise bleak existence.

She'd managed to escape, earning a scholarship to a prestigious university far away from the drugs, violence, and despair that had defined her early years. At college, she thrived, immersing herself in her studies and building a future that seemed worlds away from the life she had left behind. She was on the verge of graduating with honors, ready to embark on a promising career.

But life had a way of throwing curveballs. One lapse in judgment, a moment of weakness, and everything she had worked for was jeopardized. Now, she was back, forced to return to the place she had fought so hard to escape, harboring a secret that could shatter her carefully constructed world.

The moment she stepped onto her old block, heads turned. Eyes followed her every move, whispers spreading like wildfire. "Ain't that Ranisha Barlow? Thought she left for good."

Ranisha ignored the stares, her head held high. She wasn't here to engage in gossip or relive old memories. She had a mission, and she intended to see it through. As she walked, she noticed how little had changed. The same faces loitered on the corners, the same sounds of children playing and adults arguing filled the air.

Her first stop was her mother's house. The small, dilapidated building stood as a testament to the hard years they had endured. She knocked on the door, her heart pounding. The door creaked open, and her mother's weary face appeared. For a moment, they just looked at each other, the silence heavy with unspoken words.

"Ranisha," her mother finally said, her voice a mix of surprise and relief. "What are you doing here?"

Ranisha forced a smile. "Hey, Ma. I needed to come back. Can I come in?"

Her mother stepped aside, letting her in. The inside of the house was as she remembered—modest, but clean and filled with love. They sat down in the cramped living room, the weight of Ranisha's secret pressing down on her.

As the news of her return spread, it wasn't long before the neighborhood grapevine kicked into high gear. Every corner she turned, she was met with curious eyes and probing questions. Old friends and acquaintances wanted to know what had brought her back, but Ranisha was careful with her answers, deflecting with vague responses.

Despite her attempts to keep a low profile, it was inevitable that she would run into Pierre "P" Jones. Their paths had crossed many times during her childhood. Pierre had started from the bottom, just like everyone else, but he had clawed his way to the top of the local underworld. His fast lifestyle and power had made him a figure of both fear and admiration in the neighborhood.

Ranisha had always been an enigma to him. He admired her drive and ambition, but their lives had taken such different paths that he never thought they would cross again. When he heard she was back, his curiosity was piqued. What could have brought Ranisha Barlow, the girl who was supposed to make it out, back to the hood?

Their meeting was inevitable. Ranisha was walking down the street when she heard the unmistakable roar of Pierre's car. He pulled up beside her, rolling down the window with a smirk. "Well, if it isn't Miss Barlow. Didn't think I'd see you back around here."

Ranisha forced a smile, her heart racing. "Hello, Pierre. It's been a while."

Pierre got out of the car, leaning against it casually. "Yeah, it has. So, what brings you back to our humble little corner of the world?"

Ranisha shrugged, trying to keep her tone light. "Just some family stuff. Needed to take care of a few things."

Pierre studied her for a moment, his eyes narrowing. "Family stuff, huh? You know, people talk. Word is you've been doing big things. So why come back now?"

Ranisha felt a pang of fear. She couldn't let him or anyone else see through her façade. "Sometimes, you just have to come home, right?"

Pierre nodded slowly, clearly not convinced but willing to let it slide for now. "Well, if you need anything, you know where to find me."

Ranisha watched him drive away, her heart heavy. She had returned with a purpose, but the shadows of her past were already closing in. Her secret was a ticking time bomb, and she knew it was only a matter of time before it all came crashing down.

As she walked back to her mother's house, the weight of her situation settled over her. She had fought so hard to leave this life behind, but now she was back, and the stakes were higher than ever. Ranisha was determined to face whatever came her way, but the path ahead was fraught with danger and uncertainty. The streets had a way of pulling you back in, no matter how far you ran.

Chapter 2: Unfinished Business

Pierre "P" Jones stood on the balcony of his penthouse apartment, overlooking the sprawling neighborhood he controlled. From these heights, he could see the entire empire he had built from the ground up. He remembered the days when he had nothing, hustling on these same streets, dreaming of the power he now held. Life had taught him hard lessons, and he had learned them well.

Pierre was known throughout the hood as a man who didn't take no for an answer. He was ruthless in his rise to power, earning respect and fear in equal measure. His presence was commanding, his reputation solidified by years of strategic moves and unyielding determination. The streets respected strength, and Pierre embodied it.

His phone buzzed, snapping him out of his reverie. It was a message from one of his boys, letting him know that Ranisha was back in town. The name brought back a flood of memories, and Pierre felt a mix of emotions stir within him. Ranisha had been different from all the other girls. She had fire, ambition, and a drive that matched his own. Their time together had been intense, passionate, and ultimately, painful.

Ranisha and Pierre had been inseparable at one time. They were both driven, both hungry for a life beyond the constraints of their upbringing. But where Pierre embraced the streets, Ranisha sought escape through education. Their paths had diverged, leading to a heated breakup. Ranisha had left, determined to carve out a future far removed from Pierre's world of crime and chaos.

But despite their differences, the connection between them had never truly faded. There was a time when Ranisha saw the softer side of Pierre, the side he rarely showed to anyone else. He had protected her, supported her dreams, and in turn, she had seen the potential in him beyond the violence and ambition. Their breakup had been devastating for both, filled with harsh words and broken promises.

That evening, Pierre decided to pay a visit to the old block. His crew followed closely behind, a silent testament to his authority. As he approached, he saw Ranisha coming out of the store. She looked the same, yet different. Stronger, more resolved, but still the same fire in her eyes.

He pulled up to the store with music blasting he parked right in front of Ranisha and got out trying to grab her attention. "Back in the hood like old times."

Ranisha stopped, her heart racing at the sight of him. "Pierre. Still rolling around with an entourage, I see."

"Gotta keep my business safe, you know how it is."

Ranisha nodded, a mix of emotions churning inside her. "Yeah, I remember. You always had a way of keeping things... under control."

Their eyes locked, the tension between them palpable. The memories of their past hung in the air, both of them recalling the passion and the pain they had shared. Pierre took a step closer, his gaze intense. "You never did tell me why you left."

Ranisha sighed, looking away. "I had to get out, Pierre. Had to make something of myself. Couldn't do that here."

Pierre frowned, his frustration evident. "And now you're back. What happened, Ranisha? What brought you back?"

She hesitated, the weight of her secret pressing down on her. "Just some unfinished business. That's all."

Pierre studied her for a moment, sensing there was more to the story. But he knew better than to push too hard. "Well, whatever it is, you know where to find me. Just remember, this place hasn't changed. It's still dangerous."

Ranisha nodded, feeling a mixture of comfort and fear. "I know, Pierre. I haven't forgotten."

As they parted ways, Ranisha felt the old emotions stirring within her. Despite everything, there was a part of her that had never stopped caring for Pierre. But she couldn't let herself get drawn back into his world. She had a secret to protect, and her future depended on it.

Pierre watched her go, his mind racing with thoughts of the past and the present. Ranisha's return had stirred something in him, something he hadn't felt in a long time. He was determined to find out what had brought her back, and he wasn't going to lose her again.

The streets buzzed with the news of their encounter. Gossip spread like wildfire, people speculating about the nature of their meeting and what it meant for the neighborhood. Ranisha's return had already caused a stir, and now, with Pierre involved, things were bound to get even more complicated.

Ranisha returned to her mother's house, her mind in turmoil. She knew that being back in the hood meant facing her past, but she hadn't expected it to be this intense. Pierre was a force to be reckoned with, and she couldn't afford to let her guard down.

As the night fell, Ranisha lay in bed, the weight of her secret pressing down on her. She knew she couldn't keep it hidden forever, and the thought of Pierre finding out terrified her. But she had no choice. She had to stay strong, for herself and for those she cared about.

The next day, Ranisha woke with a renewed sense of determination. She couldn't let her past define her future. She had to face whatever came her way, no matter how difficult. And she had to do it on her own terms.

As she stepped out into the streets once more, Ranisha knew that her journey was far from over. The road ahead was filled with challenges and dangers, but she was ready to face them head-on. She had unfinished business to attend to, and she wasn't going to let anything stand in her way.

Chapter 3: Hidden Agendas

Ranisha sat in her mother's cramped kitchen, staring at the old tablecloth with its faded patterns. She had been back in the neighborhood for only a few days, but the pressure of her secret was already weighing heavily on her. She stirred her coffee absently, her mind racing with thoughts of how to rebuild her life without letting anyone find out why she had returned.

Her mother, ever perceptive, watched her with concern. "You alright, baby? You seem a little off."

Ranisha forced a smile. "I'm fine, Ma. Just got a lot on my mind, that's all."

Her mother nodded but didn't press further. She knew better than to push Ranisha when she wasn't ready to talk. "Just remember, you don't have to carry everything on your own."

Ranisha's smile faltered. If only it were that simple. She had spent years running from her past, and now she was back, trying to build a future while hiding a secret that could destroy everything she had worked for. She needed to be careful, to keep her guard up, but every day in the neighborhood made it harder to maintain the façade.

Meanwhile, Pierre was on a mission of his own. He couldn't stop thinking about Ranisha. Seeing her again had reignited feelings he thought he had buried long ago. He wanted her back in his life, and he was determined to win her over, no matter what it took.

He spent his days running his empire, but his nights were filled with thoughts of Ranisha. He reached out to old friends, trying to gather information about why she had returned. He knew there was more to her story than she was letting on, and he was determined to find out what it was.

One evening, Pierre found himself standing outside Ranisha's mother's house. He had no plan, just an overwhelming need to see her. He was about to knock when the door opened, and Ranisha stepped out. She looked surprised to see him but didn't turn him away.

"Pierre, what are you doing here?"

"I needed to see you, Nisha. Can we talk?"

Ranisha hesitated but nodded. "Let's walk."

They strolled through the neighborhood in silence for a while, the night air heavy with unspoken words. Finally, Pierre broke the silence. "Why'd you come back, Nisha? I know you didn't just come back for family business."

Ranisha stopped walking, turning to face him. "I came back because I had to, Pierre. There's more going on than you know, and I can't talk about it right now."

Pierre's eyes narrowed. "I just want to help, Nisha. You know I care about you."

Ranisha sighed. "I know, Pierre. But some things are better left unsaid. Please, just give me time."

Pierre nodded reluctantly. "Alright, but I'm not giving up on you."

As if her situation weren't complicated enough, Ranisha's life took another turn with the arrival of Jordan to pay a visit. She had just got the text that he had landed and was getting settled in but would love to see her the next day for lunch. He was a smooth-talking, ambitious young man Ranisha had met while away. He and Ranisha had met through mutual friends, and there was an instant connection. Jordan was different from Pierre—he was fresh, charming, and seemed to understand her need for discretion.

Jordan quickly became a regular part of Ranisha's life. They spent time together, sharing dreams and aspirations. But Jordan had his own ambitions, and he saw Ranisha as someone who could help him climb the social ladder. He wasn't aware of her past with Pierre or the secret she was hiding, but he sensed that there was more to her story.

The next day, as Ranisha and Jordan sat in a local diner, she noticed Pierre walk in. He spotted them immediately, his expression darkening. He walked over to their table, his eyes locked on Jordan.

"Who's this?" Pierre asked, his tone cold.

Jordan looked up, unfazed. "Name's Jordan. And you are?"

Pierre smirked. "I'm Pierre. Ranisha and I go way back."

Ranisha could feel the tension between the two men, and she quickly intervened. "Pierre, this is my friend, Jordan. Jordan, this is Pierre, an old... friend."

Pierre didn't miss the hesitation in her voice. He leaned closer, his eyes never leaving Jordan. "Friend, huh? You better take care of her, Jordan. She's important to me."

Jordan met his gaze without flinching. "I plan to."

After Pierre left, Ranisha could feel the weight of his warning. She knew Pierre well enough to understand that he wouldn't back down easily. He was determined to win her back, and Jordan's presence only complicated things further.

The days that followed were a blur of tension and uncertainty. Ranisha struggled to keep her secret hidden while balancing the attention of two determined men. She knew she couldn't keep this up forever, and the pressure was starting to take its toll.

One night, as she lay in bed, Ranisha felt the walls closing in. She couldn't shake the feeling that everything was about to come crashing down. The streets were unforgiving, and secrets had a way of surfacing when you least expected them.

She needed to find a way out, to protect herself and those she cared about. But every move she made seemed to lead to more complications. Pierre's determination, Jordan's ambition, and the relentless gossip of the neighborhood all conspired to keep her trapped.

Chapter 4: Gossip and Drama

The streets were alive with the buzz of gossip, each corner, stoop, and bodega filled with whispers about Ranisha's return. The once quiet neighborhood was now a hotbed of speculation and rumors. People had always loved to talk, but Ranisha's comeback had given them a juicy topic to feast on.

"Yo, you hear Ranisha Barlow's back? Heard she got herself some fancy degree and now she's too good for the hood," a woman muttered to her friend as they stood outside the local grocery store.

"Yeah, but she ain't too good to come running back when she got problems. Bet you she messed up big time," her friend replied, rolling her eyes.

The chatter continued, each retelling of Ranisha's story more embellished than the last. It wasn't long before the streets were filled with wild tales of her supposed failures and secret life.

Ranisha could feel the eyes on her as she walked down the street. The weight of their stares and the whispers that followed her were suffocating. She kept her head high, but inside, the constant scrutiny was tearing at her resolve. Every step she took seemed to echo with judgment and speculation.

At the corner store, she ran into Tasha, an old acquaintance who had never liked her. Tasha had always been jealous of Ranisha's ambition and success.

"Well, well, if it ain't Miss High and Mighty back in the hood. What happened, Ranisha? Couldn't cut it out there in the real world?" Tasha sneered, her voice dripping with sarcasm.

Ranisha clenched her fists, forcing herself to stay calm. "I'm just here to take care of some things, Tasha. You sound pressed."

Tasha laughed, a harsh sound that grated on Ranisha's nerves. "Girl Bye! You Wish'. Just curious why someone who thinks she's so much better than us had to come crawling back."

Ranisha took a deep breath, her patience wearing thin. "Believe what you want, Tasha. I don't owe you any explanations."

Tasha's eyes narrowed. "You always thought you were too good. But look where you are now. Right back where you started."

Ranisha turned away, not wanting to give Tasha the satisfaction of seeing her rattled. But the confrontation left her feeling raw and exposed. The past was clawing its way back into her life, and it was becoming harder to keep her secret.

Meanwhile, Pierre was dealing with his own frustrations. The more he saw Ranisha with Jordan, the more his jealousy grew. He couldn't stand the thought of her with another man, especially someone who didn't understand the depths of her past like he did. His feelings for her were a mix of love, possessiveness, and a deep-seated need to protect her.

One evening, as Pierre and his crew were hanging out at their usual spot, he saw Ranisha and Jordan walking down the street together. The sight of them laughing and talking ignited a fire in him. He felt a surge of anger and jealousy that he struggled to contain.

"Yo, P, you good?" one of his boys asked, noticing his change in demeanor.

Pierre nodded curtly. "Yeah, I'm good. Just got some things on my mind."

But he wasn't good. Far from it. He watched them from a distance, his mind racing with thoughts of how to get Ranisha back. He knew he had to be careful, but the urge to confront Jordan and reclaim what he felt was his was growing stronger every day.

The tension in the neighborhood continued to mount. Ranisha couldn't escape the gossip, the confrontations, or the constant feeling of being watched. Every interaction seemed to come with its own set of challenges, and she found herself growing more and more isolated.

At home, her mother tried to comfort her. "Baby, people gonna talk. That's what they do. You just gotta keep your head up and focus on what you need to do."

Ranisha nodded, but the strain was taking its toll. "I know, Ma. It's just... I didn't expect it to be this hard. I thought I could handle it, but it's like everything's closing in on me."

Her mother hugged her tightly. "You're strong, Ranisha. You've always been strong. Don't let these people get to you."

One night, as Ranisha was walking home, she felt a presence behind her. She turned to see Pierre standing there, his face a mask of unresolved emotion.

"Pierre, what are you doing here?" she asked, her voice trembling slightly.

"I needed to talk to you, Nisha. This thing with Jordan... it ain't right," he said, stepping closer.

Ranisha shook her head, trying to keep her distance. "Pierre, I don't owe you any explanations. You need to let this go."

"I can't," he said, his voice low and intense. "I care about you too much to just walk away. You and me, we got history. You can't just throw that away."

Ranisha felt a surge of anger. "History? Pierre, our history is full of pain and complications. I'm trying to move on."

Pierre's eyes flashed with frustration. "With him? You think he can protect you, understand you like I do?"

Ranisha took a step back, feeling trapped. "This isn't about him. It's about me. I need to figure things out on my own."

Pierre's jaw tightened, but he nodded. "Alright, Nisha. But just know, I'm not giving up on you."

As he walked away, Ranisha felt a wave of exhaustion wash over her. The gossip, the confrontations, Pierre's jealousy—it was all becoming too much. She knew that something had to give, and soon.

Chapter 5: Secrets and Lies

Ranisha sat in her childhood bedroom, the worn walls and familiar scents triggering a flood of memories. The pressures of her secret weighed heavily on her shoulders, a constant reminder of the life she had tried to leave behind. She stared at the old photograph in her hands, a picture of her and her younger brother, Jamal. He had been the reason she had worked so hard to get out of the hood, and now, he was the reason she was back.

Ranisha's secret wasn't just about her; it was about Jamal. He had gotten involved with the wrong crowd while she was away at college, falling into the traps of the streets. His involvement in a violent crime had led to his incarceration, and Ranisha had returned to help clear his name. The stakes were higher than she had ever imagined, and the pressure to keep her secret was immense.

Hints about her secret began to surface in the neighborhood. Whispers about Jamal's situation and Ranisha's sudden return spread like wildfire. People speculated about the real reason she was back, each rumor more sensational than the last. The streets buzzed with theories, each one adding to Ranisha's anxiety.

Pierre, driven by his desire to understand Ranisha's return, began his own investigation. He knew something wasn't right, and his instincts told him that the answer lay in her past. He started talking to people, asking questions, and digging into her life. The more he uncovered, the more determined he became to find the truth.

One evening, Pierre met with an old friend who had connections in the prison system. Over drinks, he tried to piece together the puzzle.

"Yo, P, I heard some things about Jamal," his friend said, leaning in conspiratorially. "Word is, he got mixed up in some serious shit. That why Ranisha's back?"

Pierre's eyes narrowed. "What kind of serious shit?"

"A Murder. Got himself locked up. But there's more to it. Some say he's innocent, framed maybe."

Pierre nodded, his mind racing. "Keep diggin'. I need to know everything."

Back at home, Ranisha's family life was growing increasingly complicated. Her mother, trying to protect both her children, was caught in the middle. The strain of Jamal's situation and Ranisha's return was taking its toll on her.

"Ranisha, you can't keep carrying this burden alone," her mother said one night, her voice heavy with worry. "We need to tell the truth, clear Jamal's name the right way."

Ranisha shook her head, tears brimming in her eyes. "Ma, if we do that, we're putting ourselves at risk. The people who did this to Jamal won't just let us walk away."

Her mother sighed, her shoulders sagging with the weight of their predicament. "We need help, baby. You can't do this by yourself."

As the tension in her family escalated, Ranisha's relationship with Jordan also became strained. He sensed that she was hiding something, and his patience was wearing thin.

"Ranisha, what's goin' on with you? You're here, but it's like you're a million miles away," Jordan said one evening, frustration evident in his voice.

Ranisha tried to deflect. "It's just family stuff, Jordan. It's complicated."

Jordan frowned, his eyes narrowing. "Complicated how? You gotta let me in, Nisha. I can't help if I don't know what's goin' on."

Ranisha's heart ached. She wanted to confide in him, but the risks were too great. "I can't, Jordan. Not yet. Just trust me, please."

Jordan sighed, running a hand through his hair. "Trust goes both ways, Ranisha. I'm here for you, but you gotta let me in."

Meanwhile, Pierre's investigation was yielding results. He discovered that Jamal had been framed by a rival gang, a setup. The realization fueled his determination to protect her, but it also intensified his jealousy over her relationship with Jordan.

Pierre confronted one of the gang members involved, a tense and violent encounter that left no doubt about his intentions. "You think you can mess with Ranisha's family and get away with it? You got another thing coming."

The gang member sneered. "This ain't your business, P. Stay out of it if you know what's good for you."

Pierre's fist connected with the man's jaw, a brutal reminder of who held the power. "It is my business now. And you're gonna fix this, or you'll wish you never crossed me."

As Pierre closed in on the truth, Ranisha's world was unraveling. The constant fear of her secret being exposed, the strain on her family, and the tension with Jordan were pushing her to her breaking point. She knew she had to take action, but the risks were enormous.

One night, as she lay awake, Ranisha made a decision. She couldn't keep running and hiding. It was time to face her past and fight for her brother's freedom, no matter the cost. But she couldn't do it alone. She needed allies, people she could trust, and she needed to confront Pierre.

Chapter 6: Betrayals

Ranisha walked into the hotel room where Jordan was staying, the weight of the world pressing down on her shoulders. The secrets she carried were becoming too heavy to bear, and the tension with Jordan was growing. She needed a moment of peace, a chance to catch her breath and think.

Jordan, sitting on the couch, his face a mask of frustration. "Ranisha, we need to talk," he said, his voice tight.

She sighed, dropping her bag on the floor. "Jordan, I have a lot on my mind. Can this wait?"

"No, it can't," he snapped. "I've been patient, but you keep pushing me away. What the hell is going on with you?"

Ranisha felt her anger rise. "I told you, it's complicated. Why can't you just trust me?"

"Trust you?" Jordan stood up, his eyes blazing. "You think I don't see what's happening? You're hiding something, and it's tearing us apart."

Before Ranisha could respond, her phone buzzed. She glanced at the screen and saw a text from an unknown number. The message sent a chill down her spine: Watch your back.

Her heart pounded as she read the message again. Jordan noticed her reaction and grabbed the phone from her hand. "Who's this? What are they talking about?"

Ranisha snatched the phone back, her mind racing. "It's nothing. Just some prank."

Jordan's eyes narrowed. "You're lying. You've been lying to me this whole time."

Ranisha felt a wave of guilt and fear wash over her. "Jordan, please. I can't explain right now. You have to trust me."

But Jordan wasn't listening. He grabbed his jacket and stormed out of the room, slamming the door behind him. Ranisha sank onto the chair, her head in her hands. The walls were closing in, and she didn't know how much longer she could keep everything together.

Pierre had been relentless in his pursuit of the truth. His instincts told him that Ranisha was hiding something big, and he wasn't about to let it go. He had been gathering information, piecing together the puzzle, and now he had a lead.

One of his contacts had confirmed that Jamal had been framed by a rival gang. The setup was designed to get the heat off of them and they knew Jamal had no real clue about street life or how to move around. The realization made Pierre's blood boil. He needed to protect Ranisha, and her family but he also needed answers.

That evening, he decided to confront her. He drove to her home, his mind racing with thoughts of what he would say. When he arrived, he saw Jordan leaving, his face twisted with anger. Pierre waited until he was gone before knocking on Ranisha's door.

She opened it, her eyes red from crying. "Pierre, what are you doing here?"

"We need to talk," he said, "I know about Jamal."

Ranisha's heart sank. "What do you mean, you know?"

"I know he was framed. I know you came back to help him." Pierre's voice was filled with anger and frustration. "Why didn't you tell me?"

Ranisha felt a mix of relief and fear. "I couldn't, Pierre. I didn't want to get you mixed up in it. The people who did this to Jamal are playing dirty."

Pierre's eyes softened for a moment, but then his anger flared again. "And what about Jordan? What's his role in all this?"

Ranisha shook her head. "Jordan doesn't know anything. He's just my friend and knows nothing about this life."

Pierre stepped closer, his voice low and intense. "You need to be careful, Nisha. You can't trust anyone."

Ranisha's emotions were in turmoil. She felt torn between her feelings for Pierre and the reality of her situation. She had loved Pierre once, but their lives had taken different paths. Now, everything was falling apart, and she didn't know who to trust.

Meanwhile, Jordan was fuming. He had stormed out of Ranisha's home, but he wasn't done. He needed answers, and he was determined to get them. He decided to dig into Ranisha's past, using his own connections to find out what she was hiding.

As he started his investigation, he uncovered more than he had bargained for. He discovered that Ranisha's brother, Jamal, was involved in a heinous murder and was fighting for his life. But he also found out something else—Ranisha had been involved in the Gang Life in her past there were several newspaper stories mentioning her name and her being a suspect in several crimes and he had no clue.

The realization hit him like a ton of bricks. He was caught in a web of lies and betrayal. He knew he had to confront Ranisha, but he also had to protect himself. The stakes were higher than he had ever imagined, and he was in way over his head.

Back at her family home, Ranisha was trying to make sense of everything. She felt like her world was crumbling around her, and she didn't know who to turn to. Pierre's revelation about staying safe and not trusting anybody had shaken her, and Jordan's anger had left her feeling more isolated than ever.

She needed to act, to find a way to protect her brother and herself. But every move she made seemed to lead to more complications. The streets were unforgiving, and the danger was real. She couldn't keep running and hiding. She had to face the truth and fight for her family.

Chapter 7: Dangerous Games

The streets were buzzing with a new kind of tension. The word on the block was that a rival gang leader, Dante "D-Block" Martinez, was making moves to challenge Pierre's control. D-Block was a ruthless player, known for his brutal tactics and relentless ambition. His presence was a direct threat to Pierre's empire, and everyone knew it.

Pierre sat in his office, staring at the map of his territory. He had built his empire with blood, sweat, and ruthless efficiency, but now, everything he had worked for was under threat. He knew D-Block wouldn't stop until he had taken over, and Pierre wasn't about to let that happen.

"We need to tighten up security," Pierre said to his right-hand man, Malik. "D-Block's not playing games, and neither are we."

Malik nodded, his expression serious. "I got our boys on high alert. But P, you gotta watch your back too. Loyalty's gettin' tested out here."

Pierre knew Malik was right. The power struggle was not just external but internal as well. There were whispers of discontent, of alliances being questioned. He had to make sure his crew was solid, or everything would fall apart.

Ranisha was finding it increasingly difficult to keep her secret. The danger around her was growing, and she felt like she was walking a tightrope. Every day brought new threats, new complications. The walls were closing in, and she didn't know how much longer she could keep it all together.

One afternoon, as she walked to the store, she felt eyes on her. She turned to see a group of men watching her, their faces unfamiliar. Her heart raced, knowing that they were D-Block's men. They were sending a message, and it was clear: no one was safe.

She hurried home, her mind racing with thoughts of how to protect herself and her brother Jamal. The streets were a minefield, and one wrong step could lead to disaster. She also knew they had connections on the inside that could touch and hurt Jamal even while locked up. She needed to talk to Pierre, to figure out a plan, but she also knew that involving him could complicate things further.

Pierre was dealing with his own set of problems. The internal strife within his organization was growing. He had always prided himself on loyalty, but now, that loyalty was being tested. Some of his men were being swayed by D-Block's promises of power and wealth, and Pierre had to act quickly to quell the dissent.

One evening, Pierre called a meeting with his top lieutenants. The atmosphere was tense, the air thick with unspoken accusations and doubts.

"Listen up," Pierre began, his voice calm but authoritative. "I know D-Block's been trying to turn some of y'all against me. But let me make this clear: if you're not with me, you're against me. And if you're against me, you best believe there will be consequences."

The room fell silent, the weight of his words sinking in. Pierre looked around, his gaze piercing each man in turn. He knew he had to show strength, to remind them why they had followed him in the first place.

After the meeting, Malik pulled Pierre aside. "You think they got the message?"

Pierre sighed. "I hope so. But we need to stay vigilant. D-Block's not just after our territory; he's after our loyalty."

Ranisha's situation was becoming increasingly precarious. The pressure was immense, and the constant threats were taking their toll. She knew she couldn't keep running and hiding, but the danger was very real.

One night, her phone rang. It was an unknown number, but she answered anyway, her heart pounding.

"Ranisha," a voice said, low and menacing. " You better keep your mouth shut, or you'll both regret it."

The call ended abruptly, leaving Ranisha trembling. She knew she had to do something, but what? The danger was closing in, and she felt trapped.

Desperate, she decided to go to Pierre. She needed his help, even if it meant revealing more than she was comfortable with. She couldn't do this alone.

Pierre was surprised to see Ranisha at his door late that night. She looked scared, and he knew something was wrong.

"Nisha, what's goin' on?" he asked, pulling her inside.

She took a deep breath, trying to steady herself. "It's D-Block. His men have been watching me, threatening me. They know I'm trying to help Jamal."

Pierre's eyes narrowed. "What do you mean, they know you are trying to help Jamal?"

Ranisha hesitated, but she knew she had to come clean. "Jamal was framed for that murder everybody has been talking about by D-Block's crew. I came back to help clear his name, but now they're threatening us both."

Pierre felt a surge of anger. He had to protect Ranisha and deal with D-Block. "Alright, we'll figure this out. But you need to stay safe. Stay with me until we get this sorted."

Ranisha nodded, feeling a small measure of relief. But the danger was far from over, and she knew they were playing a dangerous game.

Chapter 8: Unwanted Attention

The hood was never quiet, but lately, there was an eerie tension hanging over it. The police had ramped up their surveillance, and Pierre knew his every move was being watched. His operations, which once ran like a well-oiled machine, were now plagued by constant interference. The blue and red lights flashing in the night had become a common sight, and the whispers on the street were filled with speculation about the next raid.

Ranisha sat in Pierre's apartment, the weight of her paranoia pressing down on her like a physical burden. Every sound, every knock at the door, made her jump. The fear of being discovered, of her secret coming to light, was a constant presence.

"Yo, Nisha, you good?" Pierre asked, his voice gentle yet filled with concern. He had noticed the changes in her, the way she flinched at every loud noise and the dark circles under her eyes from sleepless nights.

Ranisha tried to smile, but it didn't reach her eyes. "Yeah, P, I'm fine. Just...everything's getting to me, you know?"

Pierre nodded, understanding all too well. "I get it. But you're safe here. I won't let anything happen to you."

The police presence was becoming suffocating. Pierre's lieutenants were constantly looking over their shoulders, and the streets were filled with rumors about who would be the next to get picked up. The pressure was mounting, and Pierre knew he had to act.

He gathered his closest crew in a dimly lit basement, the air thick with tension. "We gotta be smart, move our operations underground for a while," Pierre said, his voice steady but urgent. "They're watching us too closely. One wrong move, and we're done."

Malik, always the voice of reason, nodded. "We got some safe spots we can use. We just need to be careful who we trust."

Pierre's eyes hardened. "Trust is in short supply these days. We need to tighten our circle. No loose ends."

Ranisha's paranoia was growing by the day. She couldn't shake the feeling that someone was always watching, waiting for her to slip up. She avoided going out as much as possible, but even in Pierre's apartment, she didn't feel safe.

One evening, as she sat alone in the living room, her phone buzzed. It was an unknown number, and her heart skipped a beat. She hesitated before answering.

"Ranisha, Don't Get Jamal Fucked Up," the voice on the other end said, cold and menacing. "Stay out of our business, or you'll regret it."

The line went dead, and Ranisha felt a wave of nausea wash over her. She dropped the phone, her hands shaking. The walls felt like they were closing in, and she couldn't breathe.

Pierre found her moments later, curled up on the couch, tears streaming down her face. "Nisha, what happened?" he asked, his voice filled with concern.

She looked up at him, her eyes wide with fear. "They called. They're watching us."

Pierre's jaw tightened. He pulled her into his arms, his grip firm and reassuring. "I won't let them touch you. You hear me? You're safe with me."

The increased police pressure was making it difficult for Pierre to keep his promise. Every day brought new challenges, new risks. But he was determined to protect Ranisha, no matter what.

He started moving her from safe house to safe house, never staying in one place for too long. It was a dangerous game, but it was the only way to stay ahead of both the police and D-Block's crew.

Ranisha's fear was palpable, but so was her gratitude. Pierre's constant presence, his unwavering support, was a lifeline in the chaos. Their bond was deepening, and she found herself leaning on him more than she ever thought possible.

One night, as they sat together in a small, hidden apartment, Pierre turned to her, his eyes filled with a mix of determination and vulnerability. "We're gonna get through this, Nisha. I promise you."

She nodded, tears brimming in her eyes. "I don't know what I'd do without you, P."

Pierre cupped her face in his hands, his touch gentle but firm. "You don't have to worry about that. I'm not going anywhere."

But the threats were becoming more frequent, and the police were closing in. Pierre knew they were running out of time. He had to find a way to turn the tide, to take the fight to D-Block and the corrupt cops who were making their lives hell.

He began planning a counterattack, gathering intel and preparing his crew for what was to come. It was a dangerous move, but it was their only chance.

Ranisha watched him with a mixture of admiration and fear. She knew he was doing this for her, and it made her love him even more. But it also made her realize how much danger they were in.

Chapter 9: Revelations

The tension in the air was thick, and Ranisha could feel it pressing down on her chest. Every day seemed to bring more pressure, more threats. The walls of Pierre's safe house felt like they were closing in. She had to tell him the truth. She had to come clean about Jamal, about everything.

One evening, as they sat in the dimly lit living room, the silence between them was almost unbearable. Pierre had been unusually quiet, his mind clearly occupied with the mounting dangers around them. Ranisha took a deep breath, her heart pounding in her chest.

"Pierre," she started, her voice barely above a whisper. "We need to talk."

He looked up from his phone, his expression unreadable. "What's on your mind, Nisha?"

"I am scared, Pierre. Scared of what might happen. Scared of putting you in more danger." Tears welled up in her eyes. "I didn't know what else to do."

Pierre stood up, pacing the room. The anger and frustration were evident in his every move. "D-Block can't keep up with the bullshit Imma bring to him."

Ranisha watched him, her heart breaking. "I'm sorry, Pierre. I didn't want to drag you into this."

He stopped and turned to her, his eyes blazing with a mix of anger and pain. We're in this together, Nisha. You and me. But you can't hide things from me."

The confrontation was intense, emotions running high. Ranisha's revelation had opened a floodgate of anger and betrayal. Pierre felt like he had been blindsided, and it hurt more than he was willing to admit.

Ranisha nodded, tears streaming down her face. "I know, Pierre. I know I messed up. But I didn't want to get everybody mixed up in mess."

Pierre ran a hand through his hair, trying to process everything. "We need to come up with a plan. We need to get ahead of this before it gets out of hand."

Their relationship, already strained by the pressures around them, was now teetering on the edge.

The next day, Pierre called a meeting with his closest crew members. He needed to lay everything out and come up with a strategy to deal with D-Block and the corrupt cops who were helping them.

"Listen up," Pierre began, his voice firm. "We've got a serious situation on our hands. D-Block framed Jamal for that murder on 115th, and now they're trying to get at Ranisha."

The room fell silent as everyone processed the news. Malik, ever the pragmatist, spoke up. "So what's the plan, P? How we gonna handle this?"

Pierre looked around the room, his expression steely. "We're gonna hit them where it hurts. We're gotta expose the truth and take down D-Block and his crew."

Ranisha watched from the sidelines, feeling both relieved and terrified. She had finally come clean, but the consequences of her actions were now playing out in real-time. She knew that Pierre was right – they needed to act, and they needed to act fast.

As the days went by, Pierre's plan began to take shape. They gathered evidence, spoke to key players, and started building a case against D-Block. But the danger was always there, lurking in the shadows.

One evening, as they were preparing to move to another safe house, Ranisha found herself alone with Pierre. The tension between them was palpable, but there was also an unspoken bond that had been strengthened by the truth.

"Pierre," she said softly, reaching out to touch his arm. "I'm sorry. I should have trusted you from the beginning."

Pierre looked at her, his expression softening for a moment. "We all make mistakes, Nisha. But we're in this together. Just promise me you'll never keep something like this from me again."

She nodded, tears brimming in her eyes. "I promise."

Chapter 10: New Alliances

Pierre knew that if he wanted to take down D-Block and protect Ranisha, he couldn't do it alone. The stakes were too high, and the dangers too great. He needed allies, people who could help him navigate the treacherous waters of the streets and bolster his position. He had to move fast, and he had to be smart.

He reached out to old contacts, people he knew he could trust. One of them was Big Jay, a former rival who had since retired from the game but still held significant influence. Jay had connections and resources that could be invaluable in their fight against D-Block.

Pierre met Jay at a discreet location, a rundown warehouse on the outskirts of the city. The two men embraced, their old rivalry forgotten in the face of a common enemy.

"Jay, I need your help," Pierre said, getting straight to the point. "D-Block's making moves, and I need to take him down. He's framed Jamal and put Ranisha in danger."

Jay nodded, his expression serious. "I heard about Jamal. That's some cold-blooded shit. I got people who can help, but you gotta be careful. D-Block's got the streets on lock."

Pierre's jaw tightened. "I know. But we gotta do this right. We need to hit him hard and fast, make sure he can't recover."

Jay leaned back, considering. "I can get you what you need. Guns, intel, muscle. But you gotta promise me one thing, P. When this is over, you walk away. The streets ain't gonna change, and you gotta think about your future."

Pierre nodded. "I hear you, Jay. I'm ready to move on. But first, we gotta deal with this."

While Pierre was forming alliances, Ranisha was finding her own strength. The revelation of her secret had shaken her, but it had also empowered her. She was no longer just a pawn in a dangerous game; she was ready to take control of her situation.

Ranisha started reaching out to her own network, people she had met during her time away from the hood. She knew that clearing Jamal's name was crucial, and she needed evidence to prove his innocence.

One of her contacts was an old friend from college, Malikah, who worked as a journalist. Malikah had the skills and resources to help uncover the truth about D-Block's operation.

They met in a small café, away from prying eyes. Ranisha explained everything, and Malikah listened intently, her expression growing more serious by the minute.

"Rani, this is dangerous," Malikah said, her voice low. "But I'm in. We need to get this story out, expose D-Block for what he is."

Ranisha felt a surge of gratitude. "Thank you, Malikah. I can't do this alone."

Malikah smiled. "You're not alone, girl. I Got You Friend!"

As Pierre and Ranisha strengthened their positions, D-Block made a bold move that escalated the conflict. He ordered a hit on one of Pierre's key lieutenants, a brutal message that no one was safe. The streets erupted in chaos, the fragile balance of power tipping dangerously.

Pierre received the news late at night. He was with Ranisha, planning their next move, when his phone buzzed with an urgent message. His face darkened as he read it, the words confirming his worst fears.

"One of my guys just got hit," Pierre said, his voice tight with anger. "D-Block's sending a message."

Ranisha's heart raced. "What are we gonna do, Pierre?"

"We're gonna hit back," he replied, his eyes blazing with determination. "But we need to be smart about it. We can't afford to make mistakes."

They spent the night strategizing, calling in favors, and mobilizing their allies. The tension was palpable, every moment fraught with the possibility of violence. But they knew they had to act, and they had to act fast.

The following days were a blur of activity. Pierre and his crew moved with precision, striking at D-Block's operations and gathering crucial intel. Big Jay's resources proved invaluable, giving them the firepower and information they needed to stay ahead.

Ranisha, with Malikah's help, started piecing together the evidence that would clear Jamal's name and expose D-Block's corruption. It was dangerous work, but she felt a newfound sense of purpose and strength.

One evening, as Pierre and Ranisha reviewed their plans, there was a knock at the door. Malikah entered, her face lit with excitement and determination.

"We got it," Malikah said, holding up a flash drive. "Evidence of D-Block's involvement in framing Jamal. This is gonna blow the lid off everything."

Pierre and Ranisha exchanged a look, a mixture of relief and anticipation. "This is it," Pierre said, his voice firm. "We're gonna take him down."

Chapter 11: Desperation

Ranisha paced the small, cluttered apartment, her mind racing with fear and desperation. The stakes had never been higher. The pressure of ensuring her safety, as well as that of her loved ones, weighed heavily on her. She knew she needed to act fast, but the risks were immense.

The recent threats from D-Block's crew and the constant police surveillance had pushed Ranisha to the edge. Every corner she turned seemed fraught with danger. Her resolve to clear Jamal's name and bring down D-Block was unwavering, but the path was perilous.

She grabbed her phone and dialed Malikah. "We need to move faster. We're running out of time," she said, her voice tight with urgency.

Malikah's voice was steady on the other end. "I'm working on it, Rani. But we need to be careful. If we push too hard, we could expose ourselves."

"I don't care anymore," Ranisha snapped. "Jamal's life is on the line, and so is ours. We have to get this done."

Meanwhile, Pierre was facing his own challenges. The escalating conflict with D-Block had put his empire on the brink of war. The recent hit on one of his key lieutenants had been a brutal wake-up call. He couldn't afford to lose any more ground.

Pierre gathered his top crew members in a dimly lit basement, the tension palpable. "We gotta hit them back and hit them hard," he said, his voice cold and determined. "D-Block thinks he can push us around, but he's got another thing coming."

Malik nodded, his face grim. "We're ready, P. Just give the word."

Pierre looked around at his men, their faces set with determination. "Tonight, we strike. No more waiting. We take the fight to them."

As night fell, the streets became a battleground. Ranisha knew that the clash was inevitable, and the thought of it filled her with dread. She had seen enough violence in her life, but this felt different. This was personal.

She packed a small bag with essentials and hid it under her bed. If things went south, she needed to be ready to run. But she couldn't leave without making sure that Jamal was safe.

She made her way to the jail, her heart pounding. Using the connections she had built, she managed to get a brief, secretive visit with her brother. Jamal looked tired, his eyes reflecting the weight of his circumstances.

"Rani, you shouldn't be here," he said, his voice low.

"I had to see you," she replied, her voice trembling. "We're working on getting you out, but things are getting dangerous."

Jamal touched the visitation glass with his hand to touch her hand. "Just be careful, sis. I don't want you getting hurt because of me."

Tears welled up in her eyes. "We're gonna get through this, Jamal. I promise."

Back on the streets, Pierre and his crew were gearing up for the confrontation. The tension was electric, each man aware of the dangers they faced. They moved through the alleys and back streets, their weapons ready.

They met D-Block's crew in a deserted warehouse district, the air thick with anticipation. The two groups faced off, the animosity palpable.

"This ends tonight," Pierre shouted, his voice echoing through the empty buildings. "You think you can come into my territory and push me around? You got another thing coming."

D-Block stepped forward, a sneer on his face. "You ain't as tough as you think, P. Tonight, we settle this once and for all."

The clash was brutal and chaotic. Gunshots echoed through the night, the sounds of violence filling the air. Men fell on both sides, the ground stained with blood. Pierre fought with a fierce determination, his thoughts on Ranisha and the future they were fighting for.

Ranisha's desperation reached a peak as she received a call from Malikah. "We got the evidence we need, Rani. But we need to get it out there fast."

Ranisha's mind raced. "Meet me at the safe house. We'll figure out the next steps."

As she hung up, she felt a surge of resolve. She couldn't let fear control her. She had to be strong, for Jamal, for Pierre, and for herself.

She made her way to the safe house, every step filled with purpose. The sound of sirens in the distance reminded her of the stakes, but she pushed on, determined to see this through.

The violent clash continued, neither side willing to back down. Pierre's resolve was unshakable. He fought with a single-minded focus, his mind on Ranisha and the life they were fighting to build. As the battle raged on, it became clear that neither side would emerge unscathed.

In the midst of the chaos, Pierre caught sight of D-Block. Their eyes locked, and the two men charged at each other, their conflict reaching its boiling point.

The fight was fierce, brutal, and personal. Each blow landed with the weight of their shared history, their rivalry. In the end, it was Pierre who stood victorious, but the cost was high. The casualties on both sides were a stark reminder of the price of power.

Chapter 12: Close Calls

The sun had barely risen when Ranisha stepped out of the safe house, her mind consumed by the weight of their fight against D-Block. The air was cool, but her nerves were frayed, leaving her feeling exposed and vulnerable. As she walked to her car, she couldn't shake the feeling that she was being watched.

Just as she reached for the door handle, a loud bang shattered the morning silence. Instinctively, she ducked, feeling the rush of air as a bullet whizzed past her head, embedding itself in the car door. Her heart raced, pounding in her ears as she scrambled for cover behind the vehicle. Another shot rang out, narrowly missing her again.

Ranisha's mind raced, adrenaline surging through her veins. She knew she needed to move, to get out of the open. She scanned the area, spotting a narrow alleyway nearby. Summoning all her courage, she sprinted towards it, the sound of gunfire echoing behind her. She dove behind a dumpster, gasping for breath, her heart still hammering in her chest.

Whoever was after her had disappeared, but the message was clear: D-Block wasn't done with her yet. Her mind raced with fear and paranoia, every shadow now a potential threat.

Pierre was livid when he heard about the attempt on Ranisha's life. His anger was a palpable force, driving him to seek revenge. He couldn't let this slide. D-Block had crossed a line, and Pierre was determined to make him pay.

He gathered his crew, his voice cold and determined. "They tried to take out Ranisha. We ain't gonna let that slide. Tonight, we hit them hard."

Malik nodded, understanding the gravity of the situation. "We got your back, P. Let's do this."

The plan was set, and as night fell, Pierre and his men moved through the streets like shadows. The tension was electric, each step bringing them closer to the confrontation. They arrived at one of D-Block's known hideouts, a run-down warehouse on the outskirts of town.

Pierre's heart pounded with a mix of anger and anticipation. He kicked the door open, his gun raised, and his crew followed. The warehouse erupted in chaos as they stormed inside, gunfire ringing out, shouts and screams filling the air.

The confrontation was brutal. Pierre fought with a ferocity driven by his need to protect Ranisha. He took down anyone who stood in his way, his focus singular. The violence was raw and unrelenting, but Pierre's resolve never wavered.

He found D-Block in the back of the warehouse, the man's face twisted in a sneer. "You think you can take me down, P? You ain't got what it takes."

Pierre's response was a single shot, the bullet finding its mark. D-Block fell, the look of surprise still etched on his face. Pierre stood over him, his breath heavy. "You messed with the wrong people."

The victory, however, was hollow. The fight had taken its toll, and Pierre's thoughts were consumed by Ranisha's safety. He returned to the safe house, finding her still shaken from the day's events. She looked up at him, her eyes filled with fear and uncertainty.

"Pierre, what happened?" she asked, her voice trembling.

"We took care of it," he replied, trying to reassure her. "D-Block won't be a problem anymore."

But the trust between them was fragile, and the strain of their situation was beginning to show. Ranisha's fear and paranoia had grown, and she couldn't shake the feeling that she was always in danger.

"I can't keep living like this, P," she said, tears streaming down her face. "I feel like I'm losing my mind. I can't trust anyone."

Pierre's heart ached. He wanted to protect her, to make everything right, but he knew that the road ahead was fraught with challenges. "We'll get through this, Nisha. I promise."

The days that followed were tense. Ranisha's near miss had left her on edge, and Pierre's need for revenge had only deepened the divide between them. They argued more frequently, their once strong bond now strained by fear and distrust.

One night, as they sat in the dimly lit living room, the silence between them was heavy. Ranisha looked at Pierre, her eyes filled with a mix of love and pain. "I don't know if I can do this anymore, P. I'm scared all the time."

Pierre reached out to take her hand, his voice soft. "I know, Nisha. But we have to stay strong. We can't let them win."

Ranisha pulled her hand away, her frustration boiling over. "You don't get it, Pierre. Every day feels like a battle, and I don't know how much more I can take."

Pierre's eyes hardened, his own frustration surfacing. "We don't have a choice, Nisha. Whether we like it or not."

Chapter 13: Double Cross

The streets had a way of revealing secrets, and this time, it was a bombshell. Pierre sat in his office, his mind reeling from the news he had just received. One of his most trusted allies, Rico, had been playing both sides, feeding information to the rival gang. The betrayal cut deep, and Pierre knew the fallout would be devastating.

He called a meeting with his top lieutenants. The atmosphere was tense, the air thick with suspicion and anger. "We got a rat in our midst," Pierre said, his voice cold and hard. "Rico's been working with D-Block's crew. We gotta handle this, now."

Malik, always the first to speak up, looked stunned. "Rico? You sure about this, P?"

Pierre nodded, his eyes blazing. "Yeah, I'm sure. He's been leaking our moves, setting us up. That's why we've been getting hit so hard."

The room erupted in angry murmurs, the realization of the betrayal sinking in. Pierre raised his hand to silence them. "We need to find Rico, and we need to make an example out of him. We can't afford any more traitors."

As the hunt for Rico began, Pierre's organization was thrown into chaos. Loyalties were tested, and trust became a rare commodity. The once-solid foundation of Pierre's empire was cracking, and he knew he had to act fast to restore order.

Ranisha watched the turmoil unfold, her heart aching for Pierre. She could see the strain on his face, the weight of the betrayal pressing down on him. She knew she had to do something, to show him that he wasn't alone in this fight.

She approached Pierre one evening, her resolve firm. "P, I want to help. I know things are crazy right now, but I can be an asset. Let me do something."

Pierre looked at her, surprised. "Nisha, you've already got enough on your plate. I don't want you getting hurt."

Ranisha shook her head, her eyes determined. "I'm not gonna sit on the sidelines while everything falls apart. I'm in this with you, whether you like it or not."

Pierre sighed, but he could see the fire in her eyes. "Alright, Nisha. Let's see what you got."

Ranisha threw herself into the fight with a newfound strength. She used her connections and her sharp mind to help Pierre track down Rico. Her loyalty and determination impressed Pierre, and he found himself relying on her more and more.

Together, they pieced together Rico's movements, following the trail of betrayal. It wasn't long before they cornered him in an abandoned building on the outskirts of town. The confrontation was intense, the air thick with tension.

Pierre stepped forward, his gun trained on Rico. "You got anything to say for yourself, traitor?"

Rico's eyes darted around, looking for an escape. "P, it's not what you think. I was just trying to survive."

Pierre's expression hardened. "Survive? You sold us out, Rico. You put all of us in danger."

Rico's desperation was palpable. "I had no choice! They would've killed me if I didn't cooperate."

Pierre's finger tightened on the trigger. "And now you're gonna pay for it."

Before Pierre could pull the trigger, Ranisha stepped forward. "Wait, P. We need him alive. He's got information we can use."

Pierre looked at her, his eyes questioning. "You sure about this, Nisha?"

Ranisha nodded, her gaze unwavering. "Yeah, I'm sure. We can get more out of him alive than dead."

Pierre lowered his gun, his eyes still locked on Rico. "Alright. But if he steps outta line, he's done."

Back at the safe house, Pierre and Ranisha interrogated Rico, extracting valuable information about D-Block's operations. The betrayal had been a harsh blow, but they were turning it to their advantage. Ranisha's role in the operation earned her Pierre's renewed trust and respect.

The chaos within Pierre's organization began to settle as they regrouped and refocused. Ranisha's strength and loyalty had been a beacon of hope, and Pierre found himself leaning on her more than ever.

One night, as they sat together, Pierre looked at Ranisha, his eyes filled with gratitude. "I don't know what I'd do without you, Nisha. You've been my rock through all of this."

Ranisha smiled, her heart swelling with emotion. "We're in this together, P. I'll always have your back."

Chapter 14: Ultimate Showdown

Pierre sat at the worn wooden table, the map of the city spread out before him, marked with red and blue lines denoting territories and known hideouts. The dim light of the single overhead bulb cast long shadows, accentuating the tension in the room. Ranisha stood beside him, her eyes scanning the map, her mind racing with the stakes of their plan.

"We need to hit them where it hurts," Pierre said, his voice low and filled with resolve.. We can't take them all out at once, but we can cripple their operations."

Ranisha nodded, her eyes fierce. "We take out their main stash house and their top lieutenants. Cut off the head, and the body will fall."

Pierre looked at her, his expression one of grim determination. "You ready for this, Nisha? It's gonna get ugly."

Ranisha met his gaze, her voice steady. "I've been ready. Let's do this."

The plan was set in motion. Pierre's crew assembled in the shadows, each member fully aware of the gravity of the situation. The air was thick with anticipation, the scent of impending violence lingering like a storm cloud ready to burst.

Pierre addressed his men, his voice commanding attention. "Tonight, we take back what's ours. D-Block's been doing bullshit for too long. No more. We hit them hard and fast. Leave no room for mercy."

The crew responded with grim nods, their loyalty to Pierre and the cause unshakable. They moved out, each step deliberate, the night shrouding their movements.

The stash house was a fortress, but Pierre's intel had given them an edge. They knew the weak points, the guard rotations, and the escape routes.

As they approached, Pierre signaled for silence. The crew fanned out, taking positions around the perimeter.

Ranisha, armed and ready, stayed close to Pierre. She could feel her heart pounding, but she pushed the fear aside. This was it. The ultimate showdown.

Pierre signaled the attack, and all hell broke loose. The crew stormed the stash house, gunfire erupting in a deafening cacophony. The clash was brutal and relentless, each side fighting with a desperation born of survival.

Ranisha moved with precision, her training and instincts guiding her through the chaos. She took down enemies with a cold efficiency, her focus unwavering. But the violence was overwhelming, the stakes higher than she had ever imagined.

Inside the stash house, Pierre confronted D-Block's top lieutenants. The fight was vicious, a raw display of strength and skill. Pierre fought like a man possessed, each punch, each bullet, a testament to his determination to protect his empire and the woman he loved.

Ranisha found herself face to face with one of D-Block's enforcers, a hulking figure with a cruel smile. The fight was brutal, every move a struggle for dominance. But Ranisha's resolve was unbreakable. She fought with everything she had, driven by the need to protect Pierre and secure their future.

As the battle raged on, the sounds of violence echoed through the night. Pierre and Ranisha moved through the chaos, their focus unyielding. They fought side by side, their trust in each other unspoken but absolute.

The tide of the battle began to turn in their favor, but not without cost. Pierre's crew sustained heavy losses, each fallen comrade a blow to their hearts. But they pressed on, their resolve unbroken.

In the final moments of the showdown, Pierre faced two men and squared off, their hatred palpable. The fight was ferocious, each blow a culmination of their bitter rivalry.

"You shoulda stayed outta my way, P," one man snarled, his eyes filled with rage.

Pierre's response was a cold, determined glare. "You messed with the wrong people.

The fight was brutal, but Pierre's determination and skill proved superior.

As the dust settled, the reality of their victory set in. Pierre stood over several lifeless bodies, the weight of the moment heavy on his shoulders. The battle was won, but the cost had been high.

Ranisha approached, her eyes reflecting the same mixture of relief and sorrow. " It's over."

Pierre nodded, his gaze distant. "Yeah, almost."

The crew gathered around, their numbers diminished but their spirits unbroken. They had emerged victorious, but the losses they had sustained were a stark reminder of the brutality of their world.

Chapter 15: The Aftermath

The sun rose slowly over the city, casting a harsh light on the aftermath of the battle. The streets were eerily quiet, the echoes of violence lingering in the air. Pierre and Ranisha sat in the safe house, their bodies battered and bruised, the weight of their victory heavy on their minds.

Pierre winced as he tried to adjust his position on the couch, the pain from his wounds a constant reminder of the night's events. Ranisha, her face marked with cuts and bruises, sat beside him, her eyes distant as she replayed the fight in her mind.

"We made it," Pierre said, his voice rough with exhaustion. "But it came at a cost."

Ranisha nodded, her thoughts a whirlwind of emotions. "We lost a lot of good people, P. It's hard to feel like we won."

The physical toll was apparent, but the emotional scars ran deeper. The violence, the loss, the constant danger—they had taken their toll on both of them. They sat in silence, the weight of their choices pressing down on them.

Ranisha found herself lost in thought, reflecting on the path that had led her here. She had always been determined to rise above the streets, to make a better life for herself and her family. But the choices she had made had brought her back into the very world she had tried to escape.

She thought of Jamal, still locked away, and the promise she had made to clear his name. She thought of the sacrifices she had made, the battles fought, and the lives lost.

Her mind drifted to Pierre, the man who had been both a protector and a source of turmoil in her life. They had fought side by side, their bond forged in the heat of battle. But the cost had been high, and she wondered if they could ever find peace.

Pierre watched Ranisha, sensing the turmoil within her. He knew the toll the fight had taken on her, both physically and emotionally. He felt a surge of guilt, knowing that his world had pulled her back into the chaos she had tried to leave behind.

He reached out, taking her hand in his. "We're gonna get through this, Nisha. We just need time."

Ranisha looked at him, her eyes filled with a mixture of pain and determination. "I know, P. But sometimes I wonder if it's all worth it. The violence, the loss—it feels like it never ends."

Pierre squeezed her hand, his grip firm and reassuring. "We've been through hell, but we're still here. We can make something better out of this. We just gotta believe it."

As the days passed, Pierre and Ranisha began the slow process of healing. They tended to their wounds, both physical and emotional, and started to rebuild their lives. The safe house became a sanctuary, a place where they could find some semblance of peace.

Ranisha found solace in the small routines of daily life, the simple tasks that grounded her in the present. She spent time reflecting on her choices, the path she had taken, and the future she wanted to create.

She knew that she couldn't change the past, but she could make different choices moving forward. She could find a way to honor the sacrifices made, to build a life that was worth the struggle.

Pierre, too, found himself reflecting on his life. He had built an empire from nothing, fought tooth and nail to protect it, but at what cost? The violence, the betrayals, the constant danger—it had all taken a toll on his soul.

He looked at Ranisha, seeing in her a strength that mirrored his own. They had fought together, suffered together, and now, they had the chance to heal together.

"We've been through a lot, Nisha," Pierre said one evening, his voice soft. "But I believe we can find a way to move forward. Together."

Ranisha nodded, her eyes filled with a newfound resolve. "We can, P. We just have to take it one day at a time."

As they started to make peace with their past, Pierre and Ranisha found themselves growing closer. The bond forged in battle had become something deeper, a connection built on trust and shared experiences.

They talked late into the night, sharing their fears, their hopes, their dreams. They found comfort in each other, a sense of understanding that only they could provide.

"We've been through hell, but we're still standing," Ranisha said one night, her voice filled with determination. "We can build something better, P. We just have to believe in it."

Pierre nodded, his heart swelling with a mixture of hope and determination. "We will, Nisha. We'll make something better out of all this. I promise."

Chapter 16: Planning the Future

The morning sun cast a soft glow over the city, a stark contrast to the dark chaos that had consumed their lives for so long. Pierre and Ranisha sat at the small kitchen table in the safe house, the remnants of breakfast scattered around them. The air was thick with unspoken words and heavy with the weight of their past.

Pierre leaned back in his chair, his eyes fixed on Ranisha. "We need to talk about what's next, Nisha. This life... it ain't sustainable."

Ranisha nodded, her gaze steady. "I've been thinking the same thing, P. We need to get out, start fresh somewhere far away from all this."

Pierre sighed, rubbing his temples. "It ain't gonna be easy. D-Block's crew might be weakened, but they ain't gone. And the cops... they're still watching us."

Ranisha reached across the table, taking his hand in hers. "I know it's risky, but we gotta try. We can't keep living like this, always looking over our shoulders."

Pierre squeezed her hand, a small smile playing on his lips. "You're right. We've survived too much to not give ourselves a shot at a real life. But we need a plan."

The next few days were a whirlwind of planning and preparation. Pierre and Ranisha worked tirelessly, setting plans in motion to leave the streets behind. They liquidated assets, funneled money through clean channels, and made arrangements to disappear without a trace.

Pierre contacted an old friend, Marcus, who had left the life of crime and started anew in another city. Marcus had connections that could help them start over, and Pierre trusted him implicitly.

"Marcus is solid," Pierre assured Ranisha as they packed their belongings. "He'll help us get settled and keep our past buried."

Ranisha nodded, feeling a mixture of excitement and fear. The idea of a new beginning was exhilarating, but the risks were ever-present. "What about Jamal? We can't leave him behind."

Pierre paused, thinking. "We'll get him out, Nisha. I promise. But we need to get ourselves set up first, make sure we're safe. Then we'll work on clearing his name from a distance."

Ranisha's eyes filled with determination. "Alright. But we don't abandon him. He's family."

—-

As they prepared to leave, Pierre and Ranisha found their relationship growing stronger. The shared goal of a new life brought them closer, and the trust they had built through countless battles was now their foundation.

One evening, as they sat on the balcony, looking out over the city, Ranisha leaned into Pierre, her voice soft. "I never thought we'd get here, P. It feels almost surreal."

Pierre wrapped his arm around her, pulling her close. "We've been through hell and back, Nisha. But we're still standing. And now, we get to build something better."

Ranisha smiled, a sense of peace settling over her. "I'm ready for it. Ready to leave all this behind and just... live."

The night before they were set to leave, Pierre called a final meeting with his closest crew members. The safe house was filled with a mix of anticipation and sorrow. They were saying goodbye to the only life they had known, but they were ready for something new.

"Y'all been with me through thick and thin," Pierre began, his voice steady. "But it's time for me and Ranisha to bounce, start fresh somewhere else. I need y'all to keep holding it down here, keep our people safe."

Malik stepped forward, his expression serious. "We got you, P. You've led us through the worst, and we'll keep things tight here. You and Nisha go build that new life."

Pierre nodded, gratitude in his eyes. "Thank you, Malik. Y'all take care of each other."

The next morning, Pierre and Ranisha left the safe house for the last time. Their bags were packed, their plans set in motion. As they drove away, the city fading in the rearview mirror, they felt a mix of relief and hope.

They traveled in silence for a while, the weight of their journey heavy but bearable. Pierre glanced over at Ranisha, a sense of pride swelling in his chest. "We're really doing this, Nisha."

Ranisha smiled, reaching over to take his hand. "Yeah, P. We are. And it's gonna be alright."

"Welcome to your new beginning," Marcus said, clapping Pierre on the back. "We got everything set up for you. You're gonna be just fine here."

Ranisha looked around, her heart swelling with hope. "Thank you, Marcus. For everything."

Marcus nodded. "You're family. Now, let's get you settled."

Chapter 17: The Final Confrontation

The new city had a different rhythm, a slower beat that contrasted sharply with the relentless hustle of their past. Ranisha and Pierre had found a small, modest apartment on the outskirts, a place where they could finally breathe. But peace was elusive. The ghosts of their pasts followed them, whispering in the quiet moments.

One evening, as the sun dipped below the horizon, casting long shadows across the room, Ranisha found herself lost in thought. She stood by the window, staring at the unfamiliar streets, feeling the weight of her past pressing down on her. The demons she had tried to outrun were still there, lurking in the corners of her mind.

Pierre approached her, sensing her turmoil. "Nisha, you alright?"

She turned to face him, her eyes haunted. "I need to face it, P. All of it. I need to confront what I've been running from."

Pierre nodded, understanding. "We both do. But you don't have to do it alone."

Ranisha took a deep breath, her resolve hardening. "I know. But some things, I need to face myself."-

Ranisha decided to visit her old neighborhood one last time. She needed closure, a chance to lay her demons to rest. Pierre insisted on coming with her, his presence a silent support. As they drove through the familiar streets, memories flooded back—some good, many painful.

They arrived at the place where it all began, the project buildings standing tall and imposing against the evening sky. Ranisha stepped out of the car, her heart racing. She felt Pierre's hand on her shoulder, a grounding presence.

"You got this, Nisha," he said softly. "I'm right here."

Ranisha nodded, taking a deep breath. She walked towards the building, each step a battle with her inner fears. She reached the door of her home, the place where so much pain had been endured and so many dreams had been forged.

Inside, the room was a time capsule, filled with remnants of her past life. She wandered around memories flooding back with every step. She went to Jamal's old room, the weight of her promise to him pressing down on her.

"We're gonna get you out, Jamal," she whispered. "I promise."

Meanwhile, Pierre had his own demons to face. He made a call to Marcus, arranging a final meeting with some old associates who still had ties to their former life. He needed to sever those ties, to ensure that their past wouldn't follow them into their future.

The meeting took place in a dimly lit bar on the edge of town. Pierre walked in, his presence commanding respect. He approached a group of men sitting at a table, their faces a mix of curiosity and wariness.

"We need to talk," Pierre said, his voice steady but firm.

One of the men, a burly figure with a scar running down his cheek, nodded. "What's this about, P?"

Pierre sat down, his gaze unwavering. "I'm out. Me and Ranisha, we're done with this life. But I need to know that it's over. No more ties, no more threats."

The men exchanged glances, the tension thick in the air. Finally, the burly man spoke. "We heard about what you did to D-Block. Respect. You want out, we'll honor that. But you know there's always a price."

Pierre's eyes hardened. "Name it."

Back at her home, Ranisha felt a sense of closure beginning to take root. She had faced her past, confronted her demons, and now she was ready to move forward. She said her final goodbyes and gave her mom a clear explanation before wrapping up her visit. As she stepped outside, she found Pierre waiting for her, his expression a mix of relief and determination.

"How did it go?" he asked, his voice gentle.

Ranisha smiled, a weight lifting from her shoulders. "I made peace with it. With everything. I'm ready to move on."

Pierre nodded, his own resolve strengthened. "Me too. We're gonna make this work, Nisha. We're gonna build a new life."

They sat together, the silence between them comfortable and filled with unspoken promises. They talked late into the night, planning their future, dreaming of a life far removed from the chaos and violence of their past.

Pierre smiled, his heart swelling with love and hope. " We'll build something real, something that lasts. No more bullshit, no more fear."

The next morning, they took the first steps towards their new life. They began the process of securing new identities, finding jobs, and blending into their new community. It was a slow, painstaking process, but they faced it together, their bond growing stronger with each passing day.

They found had a small house near the coast, just as they had dreamed. It was modest, but it was theirs. They spent their days fixing it up, turning it into a home. The past still haunted them, but the future was bright, filled with possibilities.

Chapter 18: A New Dawn

With their pasts behind them, Pierre and Ranisha moved to a new city, finding a small, cozy house that symbolized their fresh start. It wasn't much, but it was theirs. The move was the first step in setting up their new life.

"Feels good, don't it?" Pierre said, looking around their new home.

Ranisha smiled, a sense of peace settling over her. "Yeah, it does. This is where we start over."

They decided to pool their skills and resources to start a legitimate business together. They opened a small café, a place where people could come and feel at home. It was hard work, but it was honest, and it was theirs.

The café quickly became a staple in the community, a place where people from all walks of life could gather. Ranisha and Pierre worked side by side, their bond growing stronger with each challenge they faced.

As they built their new venture, they faced the inevitable challenges of starting over. The days were long, the nights often filled with doubts and fears, but they found strength in their unity. They leaned on each other, supporting one another through every obstacle.

One evening, after a particularly hard day, they sat together on the porch, watching the sunset. Ranisha rested her head on Pierre's shoulder, a sense of contentment washing over her.

"We're really doing this, P," she said, her voice filled with wonder. "We're building something real."

Pierre kissed the top of her head, his heart swelling with love. "Yeah, we are. And it's just the beginning."

Jamal, who had finally been freed, walked out of the back room ready for his new job at the café. The business was thriving, and their future was bright. They had faced their demons, cut ties with their old lives, and built something beautiful together.

Ranisha looked at her brother, her eyes filled with pride. "We did it, Jamal. Look at You."

Jamal smiled, his heart full. "Thanks to you, sis. And you, P. I couldn't have asked for a better brother."

Pierre put his arms around them, his heart full of hope and determination. "We got a lot to look forward to. We're gonna keep pushing, keep building. Can't Shit Hold Us Back!"

Don't miss out!

Visit the website below and you can sign up to receive emails whenever Rachael Reed publishes a new book. There's no charge and no obligation.

https://books2read.com/r/B-A-WXARB-ESBXD

BOOKS 2 READ

Connecting independent readers to independent writers.

Did you love *A Gangsta's Heart*? Then you should read *The Virgin and The Kingpin*[1] by Rachael Reed!

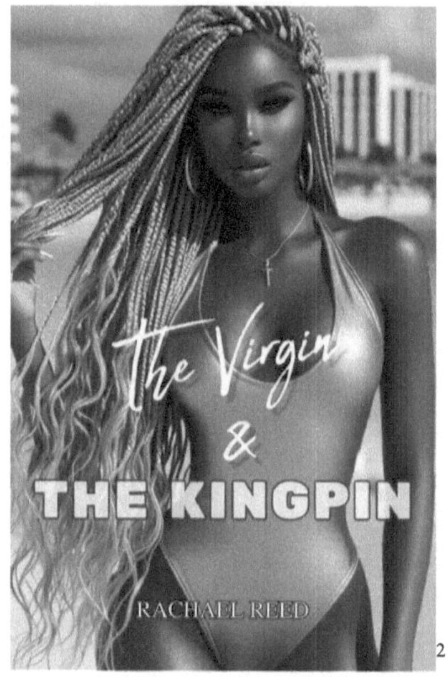

[2]

In the heart of Cancun, where paradise masks the gritty reality of city streets, two worlds collide. Megan Moore, a virgin and career-driven woman on a much-needed vacation with her best friend, is determined to escape her troubles back home. Enter Jerel Phillips, a suave, ruthless drug kingpin escaping his own chaos. For seven days, they share a fiery connection, exploring the depths of desire and secrets they never imagined revealing.

But paradise ain't forever. As their planes depart, they return to their chaotic lives, unable to forget the spark that ignited in Cancun. Back in the gritty, unforgiving streets, Megan and Jerel stay in touch, their bond deepening against all odds. Megan finds herself drawn into Jerel's dark,

---

1. https://books2read.com/u/3GlO8a

2. https://books2read.com/u/3GlO8a

dangerous world—a world filled with long prison sentences, baby mama drama, theft, murder, and betrayal.

As their relationship intensifies, so does the danger. Jerel's empire faces threats from rivals and the law, while Megan grapples with the reality of loving a kingpin. Secrets unravel, lies are exposed, and trust is shattered. The stakes climb higher as they navigate a world where loyalty is tested and betrayal lurks at every corner.

With their lives on the line, Megan and Jerel must fight for their love and survival. Will they conquer the treacherous streets together, or will their worlds tear them apart? One thing's for sure—what happens on vacation doesn't always stay on vacation.

Get ready for a gripping, emotional rollercoaster that delves deep into the dark underbelly of city living. This is urban fiction at its rawest, where love and loyalty are put to the ultimate test, and every page leaves you hanging on the edge, craving more. Can they escape the shadows, or will their pasts consume them? Dive into "The Virgin and the Kingpin" and find out.

Also by Rachael Reed

Codefendant
Codefendant
Once a Cheater
Once a Cheater
Passport Bro
What Happens in Prison
Preference
Sprinkle Sprinkle
Championship Bad
Street Exodus
Street Exodus
Street Royalty
Pawns of Power
SIS
Cartel Bloodline
Get Money Girls
Skip the Games
Til Death Do Us Part
Backpage Hustle
Link in Bio
The Virgin and The Kingpin
A Gangsta's Heart

www.ingramcontent.com/pod-product-compliance
Lightning Source LLC
Chambersburg PA
CBHW031509150726
47990CB00007B/2947